Roar's in Shorts, Let's Play Sports!

Hazel Reeves

Illustrated by Dave McTaggart

This is Roar,
the little dinosaur.

"Roar, roar, roar!
I'm a little dinosaur.
Get things ready
for me and Teddy."

Roar is brave
and Roar is strong.
She often likes
to sing a song.

"Look at me,
wearing shorts.
I've got my things
for playing sports."

Roar loves bouncing
off the ground.
Different movements
she has found.

"Up and down,
round and round.
Boing, boing, boing —
what a lovely sound!"

Roar likes kicking
with her toe.
Balls lined up
in a perfect row.

"I love footballs —
watch them roll!
One by one,
into my goal."

Roar likes races
nice and slow.
Blow the whistle –
off they go!

"Slow and steady
wins the race.
Egg on spoon —
please stay in place."

Roar loves swimming
in a line.
Snack is ready,
she feels fine.

"Watch the clock —
it's nearly time.
Lovely fruit,
you'll soon be mine."

Roar can push
the pedals down.
Then she makes
the wheels go round.

"Round and round
my three wheels go.
Hurry up!
Don't be slow."

Roar, where are you?

Roar can roll
a glitter ball.
To her friend,
hear her call.

"Roly poly,
the ball is sent.
I am happy
in my tent."

Roar loves dancing,
twirling round.
Up on tip-toe
she makes no sound.

Roar can climb
through spaces small.
Gymnastic time
is best of all.

"Lots of things
to climb right through.
Shiny slide
to go down too!"

Roar loves golf
with all the holes.
Special clothes
and flags on poles.

"Funny trousers,
wheelie bags.
I collect up
all the flags."

Roar likes showering
after sports.
She is tired,
she's still in shorts!

"Lovely water,
clean my ball.
Splishy, splashy,
off the wall."

Roar loves thinking
about her day.
Remembering all
the sports and play.

"I've got special bags
for sport.
Now it's bed-time
I will sort."

Roar likes bed-time,
things in place.
Sister's timing,
it's a race.

"Goodnight, Sister,
nearly done.
Off you go now,
I have won."

Sister peeks
around the door.
Sings a song
for little Roar.

"You run and jump,
bounce and race.
You put a smile upon my face.
Sometimes I forget to tell you, Roar,
I love you, Sister Dinosaur."

Other Roar books available from LDA are:

Hello, Roar, Little Dinosaur (intended to introduce Roar to children)
Come on Roar, Let's Explore!
Roar's Creating, Let's Get Making!
Roar's Strumming, Let's Get Humming!
Roar's About, Let's Go Out!

The rights of Hazel Reeves and Dave McTaggart to be identified as the authors of this work have been asserted by them in accordance with sections 77 and 78 of the Copyright, Designs and Patents Act 1988.

Roar's in Shorts, Let's Play Sports!

ISBN: 978-1-85503-538-6

© Hazel Reeves and Dave McTaggart

First published 2013
Printed in the UK for LDA

LDA, Findel Education, Hyde Buildings, Ashton Road, Hyde, Cheshire, SK14 4SH